JOHN BOLSTRIDGE 75 years old and has lived his life with dyslexia, a learning disorder. In 2010 after losing his wife to breast cancer, started to put down onto a computer what was inside of his head.

Although John found storytelling easy the grammar and spelling, he used in writing, would make the average person have a good laugh, But John continued, even with the disability of being dyslexic, he continued.

All that John hopes is that readers give him a chance after learning and reading this, and the disability trying to overcome the dyslexia, if just one person who is dyslexic takes up the challenge to draft a book, then my goal would be reached.

Thanks for taking the time to read this, and the story that follows.

John Bolstridge.

You are about to read a story about a couple whom from an early age had been together from infancy to the present day, John, and Janice, with them always together their friends called them J-J, John in his twenties lost his Mum and Dad to illness within 6 weeks of each other, with Johns Mum dying first then his Dad, he inherited their home and bank accounts totalling to well over £100.000.

John was always fascinated with wild camping and decided to invest in a campervan, paying over sixty-four thousand pounds, it was an up-to-date van with all the latest gadgets, we pick

up the story with John and Janice planning a holiday to Scotland, follow them on their journey, and the things that happen to them up in Scotland involving aliens.

So, sit back and strap in, and enjoy the story.

TO BE CARESSED BY A BUTTERFLY

CHAPTER 1

May the second, hot for the time of year, John outside Janice's home washing down his new motorhome, when Janice comes out and bringing John a drink telling him.

"You will wash the thing away; you've only had the van two weeks, and this is the third time you've washed it." John looking at Janice and he tells her.

"Van it`s a motorhome not a van, you can live in it full time, with what's inside her." Janice just stood there and tuts at Johns answer, then tells him.

"I think you lover the thing more than me."

"Don't be silly." John stroking the van with his hand and grinning at Janice who asks him.

"Well, when are we going to go and see how your baby runs."

"What about this weekend, I was thinking of taking a trip up to Scotland and going to see

the locks, they say it`s just like being at the seaside."

"Scotland you've got to be kidding me, they say it never stops raining up there."

"No that is where you are wrong, for I've seen the weather forecast and it said it was going to be fine for the next two weeks up there." Janice standing there and pondering at what John had said, then asks him.

"Well, what about things for the trip."

"No problem I was thinking of going down to that new shop that had opened on the retail park, called camping for you. They supplied all the things we will need, just look at the size of this."

John opening the back door on the back side of the motorhome, he opens it up and tells Janice.

"This is what they call the garage."

"Wow you could live in that space." Janice sticking her head into the empty garage.

"Come on then Babe let us get started." John giving Janice his cup back that she had brought out for him, with Janice just giving

John that look that said thank you very much I will take it in.

So, it was off to the camping shop to stock up on things that they will need for the Scottish trip. John pulling off their driveway, and off to the camping shop on the retail park, john pulls into the retail park and pulls up outside the shop telling Janice.

"Well, here we are babe, I've parked here so we can load up when we have finished, and not have far to walk to the van."

"What are you talking about, what are you mainly looking for."

Janice getting out of the van and waiting for an answer.

"Well firstly we will need a picnic set, you know table and four chairs."

"Why four there is only two of us."

"You never know, we might meet a couple of friends on the way. And do not forget we must call into the supermarket after, to stock up on beer for the trip." Janice tutting at John and telling him.

"By the time you have finished we will need a trailer to pull all of the things you intend to get."

"Don't be silly, the garage will be sufficient, you wait and see." They spend about an hour inside the shop, John buying this and that, camping barbeque set table and chairs, you name it John gets it, and finally at the checkout Janice's eyes light up at the price john had paid for the goods he brought for the trip.

"Gosh John you've spent over £400, it would have been easy to just book into an hotel, for that price."

"Nay lass in a hotel you would not have the fresh air and sitting out in the wild, having a drink, and the scenery has well, no it`s well worth the price. Come on supermarket next, and if you like you can pay if you are that keen." John pushing the flatbed trolly with Janice bringing up the rear and grimacing at what John had suggested.

All loaded and the main thing yes four packs of beer, eighteen cans to a pack, and all their food for the trip, and the boot was full, with Janice telling John.

"Well, it looks like my next job will be filling up the fridge and cupboards with the food, when we get back home."

John pulls onto the driveway and he tells Janice.

"I'll put the kettle on, and we will have ourselves a nice cup of coffee."

"While you are doing that, I will put the things away in the van."

John brings out the coffee and by the time Janice had finished filling the cupboards, she comes and sits with John at the table and takes a well-deserved sip of her coffee.

CHAPTER 2

Six-o-clock Saturday morning the alarm clock goes off and John is first up with Janice just turning over and grumbling at John for disturbing her. John showered and shaved, comes into the bedroom, pulls back the covers and smacks Janice on the backside and telling her.

"Rise and shine on this lovely morning, the Sun is up and shining, and look at you, one hell of a grumpy gnome"

"What the hell you on about." Janice pulling the duvet back on her and burying her head under the duvet. John downstairs and making himself some serial when it to the kitchen comes Janice's Mum.

"My your up early John, can't you sleep."

"Yes, I'm fine, we are going up to Scotland in the motorhome and if her majesty rises, we will be off."

"If I, were you, I would be up there and pull the sheets off her, for madam will be in there all day if you let her." Janice's Mum telling John. John is about to follow Mums orders when into the kitchen comes Janice hair ruffled and looking like the monkey had been swinging her around the room, the way she looked.

"Come on Janice pull yourself together, we want a rarely early start if we are going to make it, for it will be a 6-hour trip."

"Don't worry when I've had my first coffee will be ready in no time."

Breakfast over and the time just after 7am and John standing at the front door, with Janice coming downstairs and telling John.

"Here I am 7am and in the middle of the night rearing to go."

John telling Janice.

"Very funny, let us get gone, bye Mum see you in a fortnights time, John shouting through to the kitchen with Janice telling her the same. Janice's Mum comes out of the kitchen and waves to them both.

They both get into the motorhome and John putting his seat belt on and setting the sat-nav, with Janice telling John.

"Everything is ready, we have food gas water, I don't think we've forgotten anything."

"Well Let's get going, Scotland here we come." John smiling at Janice pulls forward out of the driveway and stops at the edge of the main road. John is looking to make sure it is safe to pull out onto the main road, when over the radio comes the song by Cliff Richards, we are going on a summer holiday. Well john pulls onto the main road, and both are giggling at what was playing, for they were off to Scotland and what a song to start off their journey. They had been traveling for about 2 hours and just before they come off the motorway John pulls into the services and tells Janice, do you want to brew up a drink here in the van, or have something in the services.

"Let's go into the services, I don't want a lot of pots to wash before we set off again." They go into the services and John orders two full English breakfasts and two coffees, and they go and sit down and enjoy their meal and sitting watching the vehicles flash by on the motorway. Janice picks up the recipe that John had paid for the meal, and she sees that it came to £21.50, she gasps at John who asks her.

"What is wrong babe."

"It's this bill have a look £21.50, now I wish I had cooked you your breakfast in the van, I could have done with the money to spend up in Scotland."

"There is not a lot of shops where we are going Babe." They spend about 30 minutes in the services and then John tells Janice.

 "Well lets Carrie on up towards Scotland, we will stop just after lunch, then the long haul over the border, into Scotland." Janice looking at the blue sky and telling John.

"I. and I bet when we reach the boarder, it will start raining."

"Stop being negative Babe, you'll have Scottish people after you," Janice smiling and putting her seatbelt back on."

Now it was off on the second leg of their journey up towards the boarder, another two hours and they come to the sign. Welcome to the Scottish boarder, John goes bye and starts to sing the song, I belong to Glasgow, Glasgow belongs to me." When his windscreen wipers come on and Janice is straight into Johns face.

"Here you go, we` crossed the border and what did I say, yes it`s raining."

"No, it's not rain just mist from the low cloud off the mountains."

"John had now been driving for 5 hours and he knew that they had at least another hour to travel when they were going by a public house with a large sign outside it saying campervan and motorhomes welcome, overnight stay with free parking, well John breaks and goes in and at the back of the large carpark there were four vans and he parks next to one and goes and parks up, he tells Janice.

"I think we will park here and stop overnight, for it is free.

CHAPTER 3

Janice and John change, and John tells Janice that they will have a few drinks before they have a meal, John putting on his casual jeans and white T-shirt and Janice one of her long dresses.

Come on Babe lets go and introduce ourselves to the landlord and landlady." Janice taking

Johns arm and walking towards the pub, with Janice telling John.

"I`m looking forward to this evening."

"Me too, it will be nice to have a drink and not have the fear of driving home afterwards, with having our motorhome parked in the pub carpark." They go into the pub and into the best side and behind the bar is the Landlord, John tells him.

"Good evening it`s nice to be here this is my wife Janice and my names John, we are parked in the back of the carpark and when coming into the carpark we saw your sign for free overnight parking."

"That be true my names Keith and the Lady at the other end of the bar is Ruth my wife, please to have your company this evening, what will it be."

"Pint of Lager for me and what would you like dear." John looking at Janice who tells him.

"a large white wine if you please." Janice smiling at Keith.

They tell Keith that they will sit over in the corner near the window.

"Well get yourself sat down, and I will bring them over to you. Janice and John go and sit down, and Keith brings their drink to them. He looks out of the window and asks John which be his fan."

"The one near the edge, that's mine."

"My that looks new, I bet it cost a bob or two."

"Indeed, it did, but I've all ways thought of owning one, and now I've got one, and the World is our oyster."

Where are you heading then?"

"We are thinking of going around the lakes, you know find a great spot near a lake, and enjoying the view."

"Lucky old you, wish I could just up stick and go, but then I would not have a wonderful place like this to run, but I'll tell you one thing, I've had one or two people coming in and saying they have seen one or two mysteries,' with things happening over the last month."

"Like what." John asking Keith.

"Well mysterious lights in the sky, and weird noises." John titters and telling Keith.

"Maybe they were seeing the northern lights and of course we are up in Scotland, and to the noises, they might have been the wild animals up here like stags foxes and things."

"Maybe but if I were you, I would keep my eyes and hears open at all times." John looking at Janice who looked a little frightened at what Keith had said.

"Come on babe take no notice and get that wine down you, and have another one, you will be ok when you've had it." It was a few more beers and wine then they went into the dining area and had a wonderful meal.

Back in the van they relax and watch a little tv, and about 12 midnight they turn in, for the night. They lay in bed and Janice tells John.

"This is the first night we have spent in this bed, and to tell you the truth.

"It`s quite comfortable." Janice turning and giving John a great big kiss, and we all know where that will end up. In all they have what any other young couple get up too. The next morning it is 6.30 am John up first showers and puts the kettle on and brews a cup of tea and goes and sits outside watching the sun rise from behind the mountains. He sits there with the mist rolling over the fields Then in the vans doorway comes Janice and she said her good morning to John who intakes a deep breath and tells her.

"Who else would do this, I mean birds singing, fresh air, sun rising." He hears a grump turns and sees the back end of Janice heading back into the bedroom, and we all know what she does next, you have it, she is back into bed and pulls the blankets over her head. John sits outside till about 7am and decides to make a full English, he starts to fry-up some bacon and the aroma of the bacon goes through to Janice who lay there, and her nostrils are going ten to the dozen, sits up and asks John.

"What are you doing." Well John with a spatula in his hand gives her that look that tells you he is thinking.

"Cooking a Sunday roast."

"Funny it smells lovely, she is straight up and into the shower, comes out just when John is plating up their breakfast, he asks her.

"In or out."

"Outside in the sunshine." John taking both breakfasts outside and puts them on the table. Janice joins John and they both sit and enjoy the most wonderful breakfast that they have had in a long time.

CHAPTER 4

8 am John packing the table and two chairs into the garage of the motorhome, and Janice washing the pots and storing them away ready for the off, to continue their trip up to the first lake, they had been driving for about an hour and just before they hit the first lake John decides to stop and a local store to top up with a few things and mainly to fill back up the motorhome with diesel. John filling up the van unlocks a side box that holds a plastic jerrycan, that supplies the Chinese diesel heater. John his thinking.

"You never know, it might turn cold at night." All filled up and topped up with food and it was off to the first Lake, they finally come to the lake and Janice tells John.

"Wow just look at the size of this lake, it is massive, John driving and trying to snatch a quick look, but with driving he is more concentrating on the road. They start to go round the lake and find an exclusive spot, just off the shore of the lake, John pulls onto the spot and looks at Janice and tells her.

"Wow this is great, no one around, and only enough room for the one Motorhome." Janice is first to swing her chair round so it is facing towards the table, gets up and opens the motorhome side door and to her surprise it is only two steps into the lock.

"John you could dive straight into the lock, from here."

"That will be fine I will put the table and chairs at the back of the motorhome. All set up and it was ready for them to enjoy, John stands with his trainers and socks off and his feet in the water with the gentle ripple of the locks water gently lapping up against his feet, John looks across the lake and the mountains all green with-it mid-summer, he takes a deep breath and turns to Janice who be putting down onto the table two coffees that she had made and tells her.

"This is the life, cannot wait till breakfast, for this is going to be our best holiday ever," John coming out of the water and going back to where Janice is sitting sipping her coffee.

"What's the plan for today then." Janice looking at John who looks round to see if anyone is around.

"Well, I'll tell you one thing, it's warm and I feel like a swim, "John standing and taking off his T-shirt dropping his shorts and starts running towards the lake and diving in, and just before he dives in telling Janice.

"Come on cissy, the waters luverly."

"John you've nothing on if anyone sees you. "John looking round and tells Janice.

"There's no one around, come on Babe, don't be so shy."

Well Janice takes of her top unclips her bra drops her shorts, nickers, and goes running towards the lake and shouting Geronimo, and dives into the lake with John cheering her on. They are frolicking about in the water when they hear someone say.

"Just around the corner Bill there is a great spot for fishing." Well, if you could have seen Janice's face.

"What are we going to do now John, there is two fishermen, look over there."

"They will be gone in a minute, then we can go closer to the shore and run out, for the van is only inches away from the shore, so come here give us a cuddle."

"No way, Sonny Jim, if you think I`m going to get up to mischief, you've another thing sonny Jim, I'm going to get out." Janice making a bee line for the door, and as she ran, she hears two wolf whistles, yes it was the two fishermen who did spot her. John comes out and might I say at a normal speed and gives the two guys a wave.

Both inside Janice wiping herself down, looks At John and tells him.

"How embarrassing was that? I mean two men seeing me in the nude, do not ever ask me to do anything like that again." All that John did was giggle and tell her.

"Do not worry Janice, you will never see them in your live time again. "Changed and Janice tells John to fetch their clothes back in from around the table

 the back of the van, John goes and coming back sees one of the men reeling in this massive fish, John shouts to Janice

"Babe come and have a look at this." Janice comes and John pointing to the man who is just lifting the massive fish out of the water."

"Good grieve, to think I was swimming in there with great big monsters like that."

"They would not come near you babe, tell you what, I'll get my camera, let's go for a walk into the woods and see what wildlife we can take." Ready and John locks the motorhome up and they go walking off into the woods, walking along a trail that had been made by others who had come before.

John and Janice enter the wood and John with the biggest grin on his face tells Janice.

"Now I've got you in the woods let's make wild mad passionate love like the animals."

"If you come near me, I'll kick you where the monkey keeps his nuts."

"Only asking Babe, give us a kiss instead, I love you to bits." Janice giving John a kiss, and in the corner of her eye spots a stag.

CHAPTER 5

Janice breaks away from John and pointing telling him in a quiet voice.

"Look John a stag, he looks majestic." John looks and picking his cannon camera up points it at the Stag and zooms in and gets the perfect photo. He looks at the screen on the camera and telling Janice.

"Wow what a picture, take a look at this." John showing Janice the shot he had of the stag. Janice looks and suddenly out of the corner of her eye she sees this massive thing fly up into the air, she screams out to John.

"What's that over there." John looking and seeing nothing.

"Hell, Janice, you made me jump out of my skin. For what are you screaming?

"There was this big black thing with wings, I'm sure it was a giant butterfly."

"Now you are talking silly, giant butterfly indeed."

"Well, I don't like it here, let's go please John."

"Well, if you insist will go and walk round the lake, come on then scaredy cat let's get out of here." They come to the edge of the wood and suddenly this wood pigeon flaps its wings and flies off, with Janice screaming out.

"Bloody hell Janice it's only a pigeon."

"Well, the noise it made, made me think of that giant thing I saw back in the wood." John looking at Janice with that look that tells you, bloody Woman. They are walking around the Lake and John is getting some good shots of wildlife. John looks at his watch and the time be 12.30pm and he tells Janice.

"Come on babe let's get back and have some lunch." They walk back to the motorhome hand in hand, and John tells her.

"Well, that was certainly a nice walk, and the photos that I've got are right on." Janice rests her head on John and apologies to John.

"Sorry John about the nonsense I made back in the woods, it`s just that with being in the woods my mind started to wonder, it must have been my imagination."

"Forget it Janice you did not spoil the walk, "John kissing Janice on the head, they arrive back and John taking the picnic table and two chairs out of the garage of the motorhome, while Janice was preparing a salad for their lunch, she comes out with two plates with their meal on and John goes and brings a drink out, and they sit and have their lunch.

John pouring two glasses of wine, and they sit in the mid-day Sun enjoying the meal, drink, and fantastic views.

"What do you think of the holiday so far Babe." Janice sitting back up and looking at John and tells him.

"Well, we are together alone, great meals and the view to die for, and it's not raining, Wait till I get back home and tell the girls, rain all of the time, poppy cock the lot of them." They finish their light lunch and Janice asks John.

"What are you going to do this afternoon."

"Well with it well into the eighties Why not go and have a proper swim."

"No way those two fishermen are still around the corner, I`m not doing that again."

"No, I mean proper swim, you know put our swimwear on."

Oh, I understand, come on then let us get ready." They both change and Janice in her bikini and John in his trunks go straight out of the motorhome door and jump into the lake. Janice swimming well out into the lake and John shouts to her.

"Not too far Babe, you never know what the currents are like. Janice turns and starts to swim back to shore, she`s in the sallow part and going by their motorhome are the too fishermen and they wolf whistle Janice, she know more stands in the shallow water of the lake and they both groan at seeing her in her bikini and not in the nudie, one of the fishermen shouts out to her.

"Would you like a massive fish for supper." The man holding up the large fish that they saw early. Well John shouts to them.

"That's so kind, leave it on the table will you, there is a cloth on one of the chairs cover it with that if you would be so kind." They spend the next two hours enjoying the swim and frolicking about in the water, till John tells her that he had had enough, and was going to go and dry off and cut a few rays. John making his way back and out of the lake, dries himself off, gets the massive fish, and takes it into the van and he guts and, skins the fish, and puts it into the fridge saying to himself.

"That should go down well tonight." He takes a can of lager pours himself a drink and it was off outside to catch the last few hours of the sun rays. John sits down on his chair and looks at Janice who be just coming out of the water, and sees John relaxing in his chair, she comments going into the motorhome.

"Good for some." Janice smiling at him, all that John did was lift his drink up and take a sip.

"It is not long, and Janice comes and joins John with a glass of wine and a book to read while taking the Sun.

CHAPTER 6

They spend two hours in the Sun, when Janice asks John.

"What do you want for tea."

"Well, I have prepped that fish and it's in the fridge, our about boiled fish new potatoes garden peas and gravy."

"Sounds nice, give me a shout when you've made it." Well Johns face goes from having a little suntan to pure white with being told in not so many ways to cook the tea.

John out of his chair and going to start to cook the tea when Janice tells him.

"Only kidding you get yourself another drink, and I will do the tea."

"You sure Janice I don't mind really."

"Just get your drink and get out of the kitchen, it's not big enough for two." John like a flash grabs a can of lager and is out sitting in the evening sunshine. By the time Janice had made the dinner it was 6.30pm, she shouts to John.

"In or out."

"Let's eat out hear it's a nice evening, and the sun is still shining." Janice brings out their dinner and John looks at the size of the fish and Janice had made parsley sauce to go with the fish, John tells her.

"Wow babe you certainly have made a nice dish, let me take a sample of it." John taking a mouth full of the fish and a few garden peas and tells Janice.

"You have done yourself proud here Babe its delicious, ten out of ten." They both have a great meal and both plates are bear by the time they had finished. They spend the next couple of hours having a drink and in general small talk till the night had drawn in, they decide to retire into the motorhome to watch a little tv before turning in, Janice draws the front

windscreen curtain across and John pulling
down the blinds on the side windows to make
it private from anyone on the outside, John
sitting in the passenger seat with his feet up,
by the way the passenger seat is so called the
captain's chair and Janice in the other front
seat and her legs across the two seater side
seat, they are watching a film till about 11pm
when Janice tells John,

"let's turn in, for its been a lovely day." They
both go to the back of the motorhome where
the bed be, they strip and slip between the
sheets, John comments.

"This is very comfortable," He`s about to say
something more when there is a flash in the
van from one of the skylights above. Janice
comments on this saying.

"What the hell was is it, John." Janice sitting up
in bed and holding onto Johns hand, he tells
her while getting out of bed, and going to the
window on the side of the bed.

"It might have been lightning that we saw."
John pulling up the blind on the window and
looking out over the lake, and in the distance
does see a flash of lightning, and getting back

into bed with might I say a little faster heartbeat and reassuring Janice,

"If we see another one don't forget to start counting to see how many miles away the storm be." Well Janice laying there and counting and waiting for another flash, and before she knows, she is fast on, with John the same and the next thing they know they hear the noise of the dawn chorus, and most of all the loud tweet of the song thrush tweeting away, John is first up and goes and opens the door and stands there intaking the fresh air of the morning, with Janice coming up to John putting her arms through John and holding him and saying.

"I never did see another lighting strike; I must have fallen straight off."

"I too Janice, but it`s good to wake up to this." They both stand there in the Sunshine that greets them and the mist rolling over the lake, well it was mist or steam from the warm sunshine of the lake. Janice asks John.

"What are the plan's for today then."

"Well, was thinking of let's have a little breakfast, then move further round the lake, if you look down the lake on the left-hand side there is some large mountains, I bet the view around the mountains will be beautiful."

"well come on then, I will go and shower first while you make us both a nice mug of coffee, then you can shower while I start the breakfast."

"Ok babe that's a deal." Janice goes first while John does make the coffee, and he flicks on the radio, and filling up the kettle and putting it on the stove, is putting the coffee into two mugs when onto the news comes a report of people camping in the area where John is staying. A reporter is interviewing a camper and the camper is saying.

"Last night about 11.15 pm we were woken up with flashes of light and this sound of buzzing." The reporter asks him.

"Did other people experience the same phenomenon, where you were staying."

"Yes, everyone on the site were talking about it, I have never experienced anything like it, I mean when you see a flash it is normally accompanied by thunder but this weird sound of buzzing, no it was not normal." "There you have it, noises and flashing lights here in the lake around Lock Mead Scotland, David McCormac back to you in the studio." John stirring the

CHAPTER 7

 coffee when Janice comes out of the shower, and she sees John stirring his coffee round and round. She waves her hand Infront of John who was in a daze, looks at Janice and he tells her.

"Hi Babe, I was miles away just listing to the radio."

"Why was there something interesting on the radio."

John could not tell her, for he knew it would start her off, with knowing that there was some sort of abnormality out there.

"Come on Babe, I go and shower, then breakfast and we will be off."   By the time John had showered and shaved Janice had done the breakfast, and they both enjoy their meal, John gives Janice a hand to tidy the van up ready for moving on. All packed up and it was off, John reversing out of the little cove they had parked up in, and it was off down the road and the views of the mountains, and the lake were stunning, John finds a secluded spot off the road behind some trees and parks up facing the lake. John steps out of the motorhome with his camera and is taking a shot of the mountains towering above the tree line when Janice comes and joins him.

"Have you ever seen anything so beautiful as the mountains, just look at the mist rolling along the top of them."

"And yes, just look at the lake it`s more blue and greener than around the other side of it."

"Looks like we`ve hit it at the right time of day before anyone else had found it." They set out their store and settle down looking at the lake with one or two canoeists going by on the calm waters.

Janice looks at John and tells him.

"It`s so peaceful sitting here watching the World go by, I could do this forever, beats being behind a desk, earning a crust or two."

"Sure, does Babe, you can see why some people start van life full time." John taking a few photos of the lake with his camera. By lunch time they are sitting taking in the sunrays and John turns to Janice and he tells her.

"boy it is hot, I`m going in for a swim, coming babe." John just with his shorts on goes running to the water's edge and dives straight in, swims out a few yards and shouts back to Janice.

"The waters great come on Babe." John doing the backstroke and Janice stands up goes to the edge and dips her toe in and with it feeling warm goes walking in, like any refine female would do, she goes swimming up to John throws her arms around him and spoke.

"You're right it is warm, give us a kiss." John obliges and gives a her a big loving kiss.

"Come on Babe race you to thar rock over there."

"Where abouts." John pointing with his hand at the rock, but Janice made a fast getaway from John, who sees her swimming off at a fast rate, well he just said.

"You are cheating little monkey, I`ll show you." Now John sprinting off quick doing the crawl chasing down Janice who had a head start. Janice reaches the rock first gets up onto the rock and turning and shouting encouragement to John who comes in and he too gets out onto the rock and telling her.

"That was not fair Babe, you tricked me."

"Don't be a cry baby, I won square and fair, champion- champion." John know more than picks her up and throws her back into the water, with him shouting as he dived in.

"Last one back to the van makes the drinks." John making a big splash as he dives over Janice and off with a head start over her." He does make it back first up the little sandy beach flops into his chair and Janice coming up to him and saying to him.

"Talk about cheating, what about yourself, I suppose that means I have to fetch the drinks."

"Sure, does Babe, mines a Bud, thank you very much." John sitting back in his sun lounger with the biggest grin on his face, with Janice just giving off a big sigh, and going to fetch his lordship his drink. By time Janice had dried herself off and with two drinks in her hand comes out and sees that John had nodded off, she stands there with the biggest grin looking at the ice-cold drink in her hand, then back at John who had no T-shirt on and that lovely target of hot warm skin, and we all know what happens next.

Yes, Janice drops the can of bud onto Johns chest and boy did he jump up, saying.

"What THE #### was that."

"Sorry sweetheart didn't realise it was so cold, biscuit love," Janice standing there with a plate of biscuits and one hell of a grin on her face.

John shaking the sleep out of his eyes just tells her.

"Must have dropped off." John settling back down and taking a cold sip of his drink.

The rest of the afternoon was sunbathing and watching people around the lake enjoying themselves doing what they like doing on the water. By 6 pm John tells Janice that he was going to watch the news on the box, and he will put on dinner. Janice thanks John and she sits back down and taking the last few rays of Sun before the Sun gets too low.

CHAPTER 8

Dinner over and they relax watching the TV, at about 8.30pm John goes and looks at the Sun going down behind the mountains, and he calls Janice to look at the Sun setting. Janice comes and brings Johns camera who takes the last shot of the sun going down and the early signs of darkness setting in. They are in their chairs and having a drink sitting in the moonlight flickering across the lake, when from behind them towards the mountains, this flash of light that seemed to light up the lake.

"Bloody hell John, which cannot be lightning for sure." Janice looking at John with concern.

"Doesn't you worry sweetheart, it's only a storm that is well in the distance."

"Whatever it be, I do not like it. You do not think it`s coming this WAY." No sooner had Janice said this when there is another flash, but this time it`s not like lightning but it streeks across the sky. John standing up and following it as it goes across the lake.

"You're not going to tell me that, that is lightning are you, John."

John standing and not saying a thing to Janice for he had no words that could explain what they had just seen.

"Come on Janice let's put the things back in the garage and going inside the van." The first thing John does is lock the side door on the van checks that the driver's door and passengers door are locked and draws the curtain across the windscreen.

"There that will keep them out." Well Janice gives John the biggest look and she asks him.

"Keep who out, what are you telling me, whatever it was out there is going to come for us.

"Don't be so silly, it was just a figure of speech, there is no one out there." Just as John had said this, a clonk on the roof followed by this high pitch buzzing sound. Janice looking up to motorhome roof telling John.

"Something had just landed on the roof, and what is that awful sound, like a bee or bird buzzing, it's wings." Then the clonking sound starts to move from the rear of the van to the front. Then the buzzing sounds like it is now on the grass outside of the van. They are both looking at the side door when the window in the door goes bright white, Janice squeezes John hard and telling him.

"Please make it go away John, I don't like it." Then they both see the door handle going down, and Janice gives off on hell of a scream at seeing the door opening. Then the light comes into the van, and it makes both Janice and John just freeze to the spot, for standing there was this figure standing about four feet with two arms and hands an insect face with large wings flapping fast that was making this buzzing sound. Behind it there was about three more of the creatures. John looks at Janice who just stood there and could not speak, when the creature points this gadget at them and both Janice and John go up horizontally into the air. The creature could not come into the van with the span of their wings stopping them, Janice and John go floating out of the van, they both were paralyzed and could not move a muscle, when they start to float up into the air with the four Aliens flapping their wings and following them up, John looks up and sees this bright light and they go into some kind of craft and it was pure white inside the craft, with all these little things surrounding them, with one or two caressing Janice and John. But not for long for the large Aliens were brushing them to one side and Janice and John are taken into a room that held these arms that had pointed ends. Both Janice and John are laying there, and it did not seem like they were on a table, John with his head on one side looking at Janice who be completely in the nude with these things prodding her and touching her all over. John is screaming at the top of his voice, but to no avail for there is no sound. He sees one of these arms come down to Janice's head and it seemed to press down on her. Then it was Johns turn and the same these things feeling all over John and the same this arm comes down and John could feel it pressing onto his head, then he faints.

The next thing John knows is he is lying in bed, he turns round and there too be Janice, He gives her a gentle shake and Janice turns over and puts her arms around John and tells him.

"I've just had this weird dream that there where these Alien beings that came and." John buts in and tells her.

"Took us up into this craft and did operation on us."

"What, how is that possible, you cannot be telling me my dream."

"I`m afraid that was no dream Babe, it happened to us, how do you feel."

"Fine, you say real, why don't I feel frightened, what have they done to us John."

"I don't know, I think we should go and tell the authorities about it."

John sitting there when suddenly there is a bang-bang on the motorhome door.

CHAPTER 9

John slipping on his shorts on and shouts as he goes towards the door.

"Who be knocking at our door." Then from outside the van this voice tells him.

"It`s Mr Professor Mike Doyle from the university paranormal society, looking into strange happenings up here around the lake." John opens the door and tells him to come in. Mr Doyle comes in and introduces his colleague Bill Turner, his co-worker. John putting on the kettle and asking if they would like coffee.

"That would be so kind of you, and you be." John telling him his name as Janice comes out of the bedroom."

"This is my partner, Janice; we have come up to Scotland on a fortnights holiday."

"We are looking for anyone who witnessed any abnormalities last night involving Alien space craft." Janice butts in telling them.

"We did they came and abduct us and took us up into one of their craft."

"Bill, we have hit the jackpot, pray tell us what happened." While Janice began Bill Turner stands and goes outside and is straight onto his phone while Janice tells Mike Doyle the story.

"We had just gone to bed, when there were strange lights in the sky."

"How did you see them with your blinds down."

"Through the sky lights and John lifted the blinds and there was another strike."

"Then what happened, please tell."

"We suddenly heard this thud on the roof, and this strange noise like a buzz, but very fast buzzing sound, like a bee or fly."

"Very interesting, please continue Janice."

"Well, the clonking went from the back to the front, then it must have jumped off the roof for there was suddenly this buzzing sound and we went forward to the side door and the bright light came and it was very strong coming through the door window, then suddenly the door handle went down, and I remember screaming out loud, as the door opened."

Janice stops dead in mid speech. With Mr Doyle asking.

"Please tell what was standing there." John tells him.

"Believe us or not, but the things we saw were just like butterflies."

"Butterflies, what trivial things like that."

"No Mr Doyle they were about four feet tall with two arms and with hands and fingers, and four legs."

"And very thin." Janice butting in and telling him.

"This is when we knew what the buzzing sound came from, for they could not enter the van with their wings being too large."

"Mr Doyle writing all the information down. When back into the van comes Bill Turner sits back down and whispers to Mike.

"They are on their way."

John passes both their coffees and Mike asks John to continue.

"Well next this thing pointed this round disc that was around its neck, and we went

horizontally up and I don't know what it was
but we could not move, and we just floated out
of the van, and I can remember seeing this
disc shape craft with a bright white light on the
underneath of the craft, and we just went up
and entered with it being just one large bright
light, and the next thing I remember was being
on , or floating on a table, but there was no
table, and these arms, you know like what you
see on the TV, when watching programs set in
the future with robots operating."

"Where you alone in this room." John
continued.

"No Janice was next to me, and might I say
with no clothes on, and these things were
prodding her all, it was not a pleasant
sightseeing these Aliens all over your Partner."

"So sorry to hear this Mr sorry I did not get
your last name."

"John Blackmore."

"Thank you, John, please tell me what
happened next."

"This is the strange bit, for you see I was
laying there and saw this arm come down onto
Janice's head and it seemed to press down on

her, then after about ten minutes retreated, that's all that I can remember, except that is what happened to me as well."

"Is there anything else you can remember about the craft?"

"Sorry, nothing the next thing I remember is waking up here in our bed, it was if nothing had happened."

"To me it sounds like you went through a traumatic experience last night, as far as the operation that they seemed to preform, please could I have a quick look at your skull, Mr Blackmore." John leaning forward and Professor Doyle combing through Johns scalp, suddenly tells Bill Turner.

"Yes, here look a small red mark that had healed over, all that you can see, not even a hair out of place, very interesting."

CHAPTER 10

Please Janice might I do the same."

"Fine could I have just my fringe and colour it blonde." Professor Doyle smiling at Janice, and he finds the same a little red mark that had a little scab on it.

He had just finished when they hear this van pull up and men in all white overalls come out of the van and they were all over Johns motorhome, on the roof and around the door where the aliens had been.

"What the hell is going on, I mean we are the victims not the Aliens." John looking at one of the men up a ladder taking swobs of the roof of Johns motorhome. Professor Doyle is shouting instructions to them, with John and Janice looking on with concern, then Janice asks the Professor.

"What are the marks on our head, what have they done to us."

"I`m not sure maybe nothing, but I would like you both to come with me to Glasgow University where we have a MRI machine that can scan your heads, to see if they have implanted any device into your brain." Well Janice is giving that look at John that said what. She then terns to the Professor and asks him.

"You mean they have planted devices into our brain."

"Do not let us jump to conclusions, the magnetic resonance imaging (MRI) is a type of scan that has a strong magnetic fields and radio waves to produce detailed images of the inside of your skull. You will have nothing to worry about."

John telling Janice, it is like going inside a large drum, you are wide awake and feel nothing." Janice tells the Professor.

"Ok we will come with you, when these so-called white coat men have finished, so we can lock up our motorhome, I presume you are going to take us and bring us back here."

"Of course, we will, Men I think you have enough evidence to work on, let's call it a rap and pack up." The four white coat guys do pack away their things with Janice asking the Professor.

"Whom be these guys, they look like forensic, who work for the Police."

"Professor Doyle telling Janice,

"Mine are scientific investigators into paranormal alien beings." All loaded up and Janice and John get into Professors Doyle's car along with Bill Turner and it was off to Glasgow University. They pull up in the carpark of the University and go walking across the campus and up into the main building and are taken to the medical lab and shown into a room with about four cubicles within the room. Professor Doyle tells John and Janice.

"Please use the cubicles to change into the gown that is provided, you can leave your things in the cubical where they will be safe till you come back to change." Janice is the first out followed by John, and when Janice sees John just standing with just his socks on bursts out laughing and telling him.

"If you came to bed looking like that, I don't think you would get any supper."

"Funny Ha-ha, you should see yourself, I don't think you would get many wolf whistles."

"Excuse me are you ready to go into the MRI scan." An assistant in a white coat asking Janice and John.

"We are ready." They go walking into the room and the assistant asks them.

"Who would like to go first." Janice puts her hand up and she is put onto the machine and the assistant takes John into the room where there is about three monitors and Janice starts to go into the machine and an image starts to appear on the monitors, then Johns face drops as he sees this tiny object sitting on the side of Janice's brain, it looks like an octopus with little miniature tentacles going into Janice's brain. John standing there just said.

"My God, that's not what's inside of my brain, what the hell is it doing." The assistant using the monitors said nothing, and about twenty minutes later an assistant comes for John and he too goes through what Janice had gone through. All done it was back into the cubical changed and they are led into an office where they are brought a coffee and a few biscuits. They sit there alone, and John tells Janice.

"Those Aliens did plant devices into our brain."

"What do you mean, I cannot feel anything in my head." Janice feeling her head with John about to say something when Professor Doyle comes into the room along with another suited Gentleman.

Right Janice and John, we have come to what we can only call, the reason for the investigation, this is Mr Ingram a top brain surgeon here at Glasgow Hospital, we have both been looking at this so-called device that had been implanted by said Aliens. And our findings are that it was not done by any Human technology, therefore telling us that these Aliens are for real."

"Well, that's no comfort for us, what about these devices, can't you just remove them, then everything will be honky Dorey." John smiling at Mr Doyle and Mr Ingram. Then Mr Ingram spoke.

"Mr Blackmore, I've been doing brain surgery for twenty years and never have I come across such delicate work in all my days as a surgeon, where the device is and the tentacles going into the brain, would surely kill the patient if we tried to remove it, or at least leave the patient brain dead, which you must realise the risk is too much for anyone to bear with.

"So, you're telling us we`ve got to live with this for the rest of our lives, I would like to know what these devices do, what I`m trying to say is will they be able to see whatever we see and do" John holding Janice's hand, and both are looking at Professor Doyle for reassurance from them.

"At this moment in time, we are not sure, we will conduct a few more test involving electrical devices, which is if you are willing, for without you, we are in the same limbo as yourself." Again, John holding Janice even tighter, looks at her then back to Mr Doyle.

"It's our only chance we have left, for there is no way I would risk my girlfriend or myself, for the operation to remove the device, for it is too risky, so please let's try your way Professor."

"Good, I'll put the wheels into motion, first off, we will make you comfy here in the complex, then arrange a time for the tests, which is all for now, we will see you later." Professor and Mr Ingram leaving the room. John and Janice sit there talking to each other, with Janice telling John.

"Well, it looks like goodbye Scotland, hopes the motorhome will be Ok, all alone in the secluded spot."

"I've forgot about that, I ll mention it to them, to see if they can go and retrieve it for us."

CHAPTER 11

Janice and John are shown to their living quarters, consisting of a lounge, with of course TV and bedroom. They do go and retrieve Johns motorhome and park it up in the university's private carpark, Janice and John are sitting watching tv when Janice gets up and goes out of the room, and John the same just stands up and he too goes out , and both are under some kind of trance, Janice goes into the room containing the MRI scanner, while John was examining the X-ray department, they are not spotted, so they think, and after about ten minutes return to their room and sit back down continuing watching TV, when into the room comes the Professor and two University security guards. John looks at the Professor and asks what they need.

"You`ve been spotted on c.t.v camera, looking at the MRI room, and X-ray room, can you explain why."

"What we've been sitting here watching the tv, how could we have done such a thing." Professor tells one of the guards to show them, the Guard takes out a device off his belt and flicks the TV over to the c.t.v cameras and they see themselves looking at the equipment in both the MRI scanner and X-ray room.

"Please tell if this is not you, then please tell who these be that look just like you." John looking at Janice, then back to the Professor and shrugs his shoulders and spoke.

"If that was us, we did not do it by our own will."

"Well, it must be the devices, that you have inside your head, maybe our friends the Aliens are interested in them."

"I'm afraid we will have to have security guards outside of your room, your safety and the safety of the University."

"God now we are prisoners, what next." John with the guards and the Professor leaving them, John goes to the door and opens it and see`s one of the guards sitting on a chair, John smiles at him and tells him.

"7 am two full English breakfast, with two coffees if you please." John closing the door, going to Janice, and telling her.

"We are not alone, there is a guard watching over us. About 11pm Janice and John turn in for the night, the night is uneventful, and they both sleep tight all night, they shower and get ready, and they come out of their room and the guard stands and John spoke.

"Thanks for the breakfast."

"What breakfast." The guard looking at John puzzled.

"You are not the guard who was on last night."

"No why."

"Just forget it, can you tell us where we can get something to eat, if you please."

"Across the courtyard first on your right.

"Thank you, are you coming." Janice and John do go to the University canteen and do get a full English and coffee, and the guard too. John tucking into his breakfast tells Janice.

"This beat`s cooking it ourselves."

"Yes, but we have not woken to a rising Sun sitting by the lake in the fresh air." By ten am Janice and John are told to go to section A corridor two, where the team of radio technology be. They both enter and the room is full of equipment, looking more like a science fiction room, with men in white gowns, sitting at screens." They are approached by one of the team.

"Good morning you must be Janice and John, welcome to the radio technology department, my names Ralph Backster, chief radio coordinate officer."

"What we are going to do is to see if the device that you have implanted into your brain is sending out or receiving signals, what we intend to do is put a helmet onto your crown, to see if this is so. Please who would like to go first." John puts his hand up and they start to put the helmet on, John sits down in a chair and by the time John was fully connected Janice who be watching starts to giggle, when one of the team flicks a swich and John starts to jerk like if he was getting an electric shock, they are frantically turning off the machine, when John bursts out laughing, that made Janice stop screaming with John just saying.

"Only kidding, which will make you laugh on the other cheek Janice."

"You stupid jerk, you nearly gave me a heart attack, don't ever do anything like that again." Janice intaking a deep breath at Johns antics, and might I say some dirty looks from the crew who replace their headphones and then go ahead with their experiments. John had been sitting there for about 15 minutes when all the members of the Lab who be listening in suddenly there is this high pitch sound wave, so intense that everyone pulls off their headphones and sit there rubbing their eardrums with the sound wave they had from Johns device within his head. Mr Backster asks them.

"Is everyone OK," He`s looking at the screen and see`s that when they have turned off the screening the high pitch wave recedes, and everything is back to normal. They are taking off Johns helmet and Mr Backster turns to Janice and tells her.

"You will not have to go onto the machine for We have enough evidence, to supply the result onto Professor Doyle.

CHAPTER 12

Janice and John are relaxing in their room when Professor Doyle comes into their room and tells Janice and John.

"First of all, I would like to thank you for your help, into allowing us to examine you on what these Aliens did to you. Our findings are that you have been worked on by Aliens of not this World, and the device is a transmitter as well of what else it might do, we are not sure of that, only that it is connected to your brain, in layman's terms what you see and do, they too will see and hear everything as well."

"You are telling us that we are being monitored on everything, what I`m getting at is everything." John lifting his eyes in a suggestive way, to Professor Doyle.

"I`m afraid so, my only suggestion is that you do it in a darkened room, for they have no control of the light, even if they had special lens, all you must remember is what you can see, then they will see it too." Janice asks Professor Doyle.

"What now, have we to stop here, or are we free to go, and continue our holidays.

"We've done what we needed to do, and to your question, yes you are free to leave, but any unusual happenings don't hesitate to get in touch, here is my card and phone number." Janice smiles at Professor Doyle and stands and tells John.

"I`m ready when you are John." They stand and John shakes professors hand and they go to reception where John picks the keys up for their motorhome. They are sitting in the motorhome and Janice turns to John and asks him.

"Where to babe, another lake or what." John sitting there pondering turns to Janice and tells her.

"I don't know about you sweetheart but the thought of having these Aliens watching our every move, I mean even now up there to think they are all sitting around their screens watching us, it's like being animals in a zoo."

"Well, there's nothing we can do, so let's give them something to watch, that us humans do have a life to live, so come on John up and onwards, let's try and forget about them."

"Your right Janice, tell you what, let us go to a proper camp site for motorhomes and get a pitch with a huck up so we have electricity, at least we will have company there and not on our own. John Pulling away from the university and onto the open road, they had been traveling for about an hour and a half and John pulls into a lay-bye and looks on his phone for a good campsite and see`s one on the coast about ten miles away, he inputs the postcode and telling Janice.

"This one look`s good it said that there is 100 pitches with hook up, and only £18.00 a night, which will do, and it also had a club house."

"Well at least you will have your fussy with the beer. "Janice smiling at John and telling him.

"Come on then Babe the sooner we are there the better." John pulling out of the lay-bye and following the directions of the sat-nav, they are soon pulling onto the motorhome site, and John goes and books in and he is given plot fifty-seven, John getting back into the van and telling Janice.

"It looks a lovely site." John comes to pitch fifty-seven pulls onto it and the first thing he does is hook up to the mains, so they have power to power up their appliance's and tv.

All set up table and chairs out and Janice bringing out a drink of coffee to John, and they sit in the warm sunshine, when they are approached by another camper, who comes over to them and introduces himself to Janice and John.

"Good morning my names Dan, I was wondering if you would like to come to a gathering, we are having this evening, over there next to the large AV, which belongs to me."

"Gathering what sort are you talking about." John asking him.

"It`s something we do whenever we get together, you know a few beers around the campfire, and a jolly enjoyable time had by all."

John looking at Janice who just nods her head at John, who tells him.

"That's so kind of you, yes we will be there, what time does it start."

"Around 7pm, till late." Dan smiling at them, then goes walking off and saying his farewell to them, John turns to Janice and tells her.

"You would not get this sort of offer from your neighbours back home; It sounds like it's going to be fun."

"Yes, it sounds great, I`ll have to look what I will wear tonight."

"Don`t be silly, we will go just has we are, it's an informal due, not a banquet, I bet everyone will be in shorts and T-shirt."

The rest of the day it was sun and unbelievably they had a set of dominoes out and sat enjoying taking a few shillings off each other. At about 6pm it was off back into the motorhome shower and John shave, John in his shorts sat waiting for Janice, when she comes out of the bedroom and might I say looking very fetching in a low-cut dress, and long to the floor. John looks at her and tells her.

"Bloody hell Janice, you`ll have all of the men falling in there."

"Don't be so rude, don't you think I look stunning."

CHAPTER 13

John sitting there and telling Janice.

"You look stunning Babe, and you will make me proud, to have you on my arm, come here and give we a kiss. "Janice thanked John, and she does give him a kiss, and then they were off to Dans van for the gathering of the other campers. Janice takes a bottle of wine and give it to Dan, who goes into his van and puts it into the fridge and brings Janice a drink of white wine and John a beer. The campfire was roaring and the whole atmosphere was electric, and after a few beers, the party really kicked off, with the odd Karaoke song and might I say plenty of laughter, the time by now is 10.30 pm they are all sitting around the campfire and telling each other their business, and in general small talk, the fire was flickering away, and it was dark when Dan looked up into the night sky and suddenly shouts out.

"My God look at that streaking across the sky."

Within seconds everyone is looking at this object in the sky, for what they were looking at was this bright light going from left to right firstly at a slow pace, then stopping directly above then flying off at a great speed, well this made Janice scream out, and the rest look at her, and John tells them.

"Sorry about Janice for you see we encountered Aliens the other day up around the lock."

"You are the couple that were in the news the other day, after Aliens were spotted around the lake not far from here."

"Yes, that be us, and might I say, we were abducted and taken up into their craft and operated on." Dans wife Mary looks at Janice and asked her.

"What did they do to you sweetie." Janice looks at Mary and tells her.

"Well, all that we know is that at Glasgow University they did head scans and radio scans and told us, that we had some kind of transmitting device and everything we see, these so-called Aliens will be able to monitor our every move." Dan waves his arm in front of Janice and asks her.

"You tell me that they will be able to see me do this."

"Yes, anything."

What even when you." Janice just said.

"Anything." Then Dans wife Mary just tells Dan.

"That's enough, can't you see that Janice be upset, she does not want questions that are in your head." Then another member of the party looks up and tells everyone gathered.

"Look its back, and it's just hovering above us." Mary standing and going over to John and telling him.

"John they are back, what are we going to do."

"We are amongst friends; they will not come with an audience around."

Then in a flash the thing is only a few feet above the camp site and there are people screaming and they are running in all directions to try and get out of the way, Janice just freezes to the spot holding on tightly to John and telling him.

"Please John make it go away." John is about to say something to Janice when this bright white beam comes down, and within seconds they are taken up by this bright white light, with Dan and his wife watching in horror as it unfolds in front of their eyes, with Mary saying while clinging on to Dan.

"Poor Janice, she must be terrified with what is happening."

Up on the craft Janice and John stand there in this bright light, with Janice not Dearing to open her eyes, when this high pitch buzzing sound starts to come closer, then Janice feels these tiny hands touching her, and she suddenly falls calm opens her eyes and there is dozens of these little creatures caressing her, and she looks at her hand and they are even caressing her hand, Janice smiles at then, and there bright bluish eyes and lips smiling at her, with their wings spread open wide, and all the colours of the rainbow.

Then suddenly they all flutter away and coming towards them is this large Alien holding a white ball, and it approaches Janice and John and holding out this white ball, trying to encourage them to Take it. John reaches out and takes one then Janice the other.

Suddenly they hear this voice in English tell them.

"We are from the Planet Archon, seeking out new forms of life, and you are the first we have come across, we come in peace, so do not be afraid."

"Janice and I are Earthlings, from the planet Earth, we too come in peace, but now we are afraid, for we do not know what you want from us, and these devices that you have planted in our heads, we now have no privacy whatsoever."

"Let Me reassure you that from this day, we will not turn on the receivers, but disable them, and for your sense of privacy, all that I can say is that one day you will thank us for giving them to you, So once AGAIN, let me reassure you that from now on you will never be spied upon again."

My names John, and this is my partner Janice, and whom may you be." John talking into the white ball that he was given.

"My names Regan commander of the craft Puritan. We have travelled for many an Earth year, from our Universe."

CHAPTR 14

We have noticed that you have young ones with you, we have a species called Butterflies on our planet, which look a lot like yourselves."

"Yes, we have studied these so-called butterflies they are so tiny, not like us archons, we have studied lots of your animals and you are the only ones with hands, which is why you are so advanced far more than other things on this Planet."

"Yes, we are the only ones that can do this, John with his thumb touching all of his other fingers, which is why we can grip things and make small delicate objects, the nearest thing to humans are apes, who have similar hands, but cannot hold small objects, with their fingers being so long and their thumb set further back." They are talking for a long time and then Regan tells them.

"We will now let you go, to enjoy the rest of your life, and once again let me reassure you that your privacy is guaranteed, and I profusely apologies for frightening your Partner, Janice. He lifts his hand and once again this buzzing sound and again these little aliens come fluttering towards John and Janice, and in seconds are surrounded by these little ones, and the same the little ones are caressing them. Then Regan holds up his hand and this bright light starts up, and all the little ones start to flutter up into the air, with this sound of buzzing and Janice and John disappear and appear standing outside of their van. They both look up and see the craft Puritan just go off at an almighty speed, with Dan coming across the camp site and saying to Janice and John.

"Are you all right, I mean we saw you disappearing up into the bright light that was coming from this Alien craft, are you ok and what did they do to you this time." Dan getting quite excited about the whole experience that he had just seen.

"Slow down Dan, too many questions, yes we are ok, and this time they did nothing to us, just reassured us that the transmitter had been turned off and disabled." Then Janice turns to John and asks him.

"What did he mean we will be glad of the devices." All that John did was shrug his shoulders at Janice and just said.

"I've no idea what he meant by that, but I don't know about you, but I feel like a weight had been taken of my shoulders, with him telling us that the devices are going to benefit us in some way."

It is not long and all their new friends that was around the campfire are all listening to the tales of Janice and John up on the craft, even to a point where they are all enthralled in the tails that they were telling them about the little ones on the craft and our Janice and John were being caressed by them, Dans wife asks Janice.

"What did it feel like being touched by these little creatures."

"To tell you the truth, it was fine, not like a terrible experience but a very pleasant feeling, of calm and tranquil." The beer and wine was flowing and by the time one or two of them were yawning the time was approaching 4am, and one by one they started to drift away to their campervans and motorhomes, leaving just Janice John and Mary and Dan, till even they tell each other.

"I think we should turn in, for in the morning we will probably have the press and authorities here." They turn in and Janice and John stepping into their motorhome and Janice telling John.

"I`m glad they came back to us, for now I feel more relaxed, about the whole thing, come on John let's get into bed and make mad passionate love." John with the biggest smirk across his face, strips, and dives into bed shouting Geronimo. After they fall into a deep sleep and it was 10.30am when John wakes and he can hear all these voices outside of their motorhome, John getting out of bed and pulling up the blinds sees about twenty reporters with mics and tv cameras swarming outside of their van. He opens the door and before he knows it, he had mics and cameras flashing, reporters all wanting to know about last night and the obduction that took place.

Please we have just got up, let us just leave it for an hour, lets us have breakfast and meet in the camp room, then we can answer all your questions, John shutting the motorhome door and Janice asking from the bedroom.

"What is it John who be outside."

"Half of the Scottish press and tv crews."

Breakfast over and John does go with Janice to the camp room where they put on entertainment for their guests at night. Inside Janice and John answer all their questions, on the events that happened last night, they are at it for well over an hour and a half. When Janice comes out and there is still one or two press taking the odd picture of them. They start to walk back to their motorhome when unexpected they hear this sickening cry for help, They look to where the scream was coming from and they see Mary standing near their motorhome and it be large AV, which be as big as a bus, but John notices it was tilting to one side, with Mary shouting to them.

HELP Dan is under the AV, John goes running up to the back that had claps onto Dan, who was adjusting one of the stabilizer legs that had collapse, and the AV was pressing down onto Dan. Well John like a flash puts his back onto the AV and lifts it up off Dan who pulls himself clear and John puts the AV back down.

CHAPTER 15

The first thing John does is go over to Dan who by now was sitting up and rubbing his chest, with John asking him.

"Do you need an ambulance mate; you were being crushed by the weight of the thing."

"No, I think I`m OK, how or what did you get to lift the thing off me."

"I just lifted the back up."

"What that`s impossible, do you know that they weigh over four ton."

"Well, I think it was because you were on soft ground that stopped the thing from crushing you." Dan looking under the van and seeing his impression on the grass.

"Well thanks John, I owe you my life, for a few more seconds and I was a goner."

"That's no problem, Dan, just buy me a drink to night around the campfire."

"You are on John. And thanks mate you are a real-life saver." Dan shaking Johns hand and waving to him as he walked off back to his motorhome. John and Janice back in their motorhome and John notices still press on the campsite and there is about four of them talking to Dan who be pointing to the grass at the back of his motorhome, and John could see that Dan was showing them how he lifted the van on his own, John looks at Janice and tells her.

"Come on babe we are out of here, for we will have the press swarming around us again."

"Where will we go." Janice looking back at John with concern.

"Anywhere just let us do a little sightseeing for the day. John going and unplugging the lead from their Motorhome, and they were off, out for the day. John pulling onto the tarmac off the soft grass, and he sees the press coming to where they were parked up, and he tells Janice.

"What did I tell you they are like flies around you know what." "They had been driving for about half an hour when Johns mobile goes off, and Janice's answers it is telling them that John was driving and could she help.

"Yes, it is I Professor Doyle, we have heard about last night's encounter with the Aliens, what happened and are you Ok."

"Yes, we are fine they just came to tell us that they had come to tell us that they had turned off the thing in our heads, then just returned us."

"That's fine, but what about this incident around the camp that John lifted this Av, which be one of the heaviest Motorhomes on the market, they weigh in at just under 7 tons, and that sort of weight is impossible to lift by one man." John had pulled up by the time the Professor had spoken, and John reaches for his mobile and tells the Professor.

"Well, I can reassure you that in times of dyer straights the human can full fill miracles in times of need, to me it was just like lifting up a small car, which I've done in the past, even though it was a three-wheeler."

"Well, it was not a three-wheeler but a seven-ton motorhome, even the strongest man in the World would struggle, but you picked it up has if it was a small car."

"Look Professor, we've had it up to our chins with press and things, why don't they just leave us be, to live our lives the way we want, and not be like puppets." John throwing the phone onto the dashboard and driving off. Janice picks the phone back up and asks the Professor.

"Are you still there."

"Yes."

"John dropped the phone. Is there anything else you would like to know?" There is a pause, and the Professor tells Janice.

"I have caught you at the wrong time, which is all for now, I will catch you later. "The Professor ending the call and putting down the phone, turns to one of his colleagues and tells him.

"I can tell you that something happened yesterday, and it must be something to do with the visit to the Aliens, I want a team to follow them and of cause discreetly of course, for the way John reacted to my call, it sounds that the littlest thing will cause a reaction in his mood."

Back in the motorhome John comes to one of the lakes and pulls up, and takes the table and chairs out, of the garage and sets out the table and sits down and intakes a deep breath of fresh air, Janice comes and sits next to him and asks.

"What is wrong John, you've been on edge all morning."

"I don't know sweetheart, its if everything is piling upon me." John stands and goes to the water's edge, picks up this large log that was at Johns feet, he picks it up and throws it out into the middle of the lake, which be well over five hundred yards away, well this makes even Janice gasp at the feat that John had just done and tells him.

"John how the hell did you do that."

"Do what."

CHAPTER 16

"You have just thrown a world record there just look our far you have thrown that log. Professor Doyle must be right."

"look Janice don't you start, I`m fed up with the rest, I don't need you on my back."

"Well, don't start on me, I'll show you." Janice no more than goes to the motorhome and just like John did yesterday she goes to the back of the motorhome puts her back onto it, puts her hands on the lip of the motorhome, and picks it up to her waist, and looking at John and saying.

"Now you tell me that this is normal." John seemed to come out of his mood and telling Janice.

"Put it back down, before anyone comes and sees you."

"Excuse me, do you understand now, that something is wrong with us, we must go back and see the Professor." Janice letting go of the motorhome and it bounces a few times before settling down.

"Sorry sweetheart your right, we must go and see him, maybe he will be able to help us." Janice going up to John and they stand in one loving kiss, then John breaks away and tells Janice.

"I'll go and give him a ring." John going back into the motorhome getting his mobile out of the front and dialling the number. The phone ringing and then onto the phone comes the Professor.

"Professor Doyle here, our may I help."

"Professor its John Blackmore, Janice and we need your help, for you see we think that what the aliens did has given us, some kind power. John is about to tell him about Janice when the Professor tells him.

"You're going to tell me about Janice lifting up your motorhome."

"Our the hell do you know about this."

Well, look out of your window do you see the car flashing its lights." John bending down and on the corner in some thicket he sees this car flashing its headlights."

"Before you say anything John, I did it for your own good, for I did not want anything to happen to you both, please if you agree, come to my labs at Glasgow Uni, and we will see if we can get to the bottom of what is going on."

"Thanks Professor we are on our way." John coming out of the motorhome tells Janice.

"I've just been on to the Professor, and he wants us to go back to Glasgow Uni, to find out what is happening to us, so come on Babe let's get this over for once and all, "John packing the table and chairs back into the garage and looking over to where the car be, gives them a wave, and it was back into the motorhome, and they drive off towards Glasgow that be just over an hour's drive away. The time being just over 12.30, John parks up and goes into reception.

"Good afternoon my names John Blackmore and this is Janice my partner, we've an appointment with Professor Doyle." The receptionist looks at her book and then tells John.

"Please to take a seat, and he will be straight out to you." Within minutes Professor Doyle comes into reception and greets Janice and John, he first goes to John and holds out his hand for John to shake, John obliges and starts to shake Professors hand, then suddenly the Professor screams out to John.

"Please you're crushing my hand." John releases quickly and the Professor stands there holding his injured hand. John is apologising profusely to the Professor.

"I'm so sorry Professor, I did not hurt you did I."

"A little, but not to worry, let's start to get the testing underway, to see what is going on." Professor Doyle leading off towards the labs of the Uni. First, John and Janice are led into a room where their blood is taken for sampling, next into x-ray for x-rays to be taken, then another room where they are examined by a doctor, and by the time they had gone through all the testing the time is 7pm, and they are told that this is all for today, and they will carry on in the morning. Janice and John go to the canteen and get something to eat and drink. They sit at a table and are eating their meal when Janice tells John.

"This reminds me of my Uni days."

"I bet it does, the only thing missing is the boys sniffing around you."

"John, do you have to bring it down with your sick jokes."

"Only kidding, here let me refresh your white wine." John pouring Janice another wine. At about 9.30pm Janice asks John if he was ready to turn in for the night, well the look on Johns face, was a picture who tells Janice.

"You are kidding me right, for its middle of the afternoon. "John taking another sip of his beer.

"Well, if you are not ready then I 'am, with all the prodding and giving pints of blood, you can see why I'm ready for bed."

CHAPTER 17

John a little grumpy does retire with Janice, and Janice changed and slipping between the sheets, with John snuggling up to her and they both are soon into the world of nod. The time is about 2am and Janice is awoken by the screams of John, she sits up and turns on the light, and looks at John who is in excruciating pain. Janice gently shaking Johns shoulder and asking him.

What's wrong John, where does it hurt."

"My shoulder blades, it feels like I'm being ripped apart." Janice lifting his T-shirt and seeing two red raw lumps on Johns back. Janice had a number to ring in case they needed anything, she phones up and tells them what was wrong and within minutes a Doctor comes to examining John, and Janice pointed out about the red soreness of Johns back. The Doctor tells Janice, it looks like he has a reaction to something he had eaten, I will give him something to ease the pain. The Doctor does give John an injection and he was soon off into a deep sleep.

"There that did the trick, we'll have another look at him in the morning." The Doctor goes and Janice is soon off to sleep without any other incident.

7am John is first up, and he is in the shower, when into the bathroom comes Janice and she looks into the bathroom mirror and she gave off a big yawn then opens her eyes and what she sees in the mirror makes her scream aloud, so much that John turns and spoke.

"Bloody hell Janice what the hell is up now."

Your back have you seen your back." John trying to look at his reflection cannot see anything, and once again Janice tells him.

"You have wings."

"What do you mean wings." John stepping out of the shower and going over to the mirror and what he sees makes him say.

"What the hell in all of the world are those things." John squeezing in his shoulder blades and they seemed to disappear back into his back.

Janice trying to speak, but nothing coming out, and John looking at her bra and telling Janice.

"your bra strap at the back, you have to lumps on your shoulder blades and they are red raw."

"What, I've no pain, you aren't telling me that I too, are going to have wings sprouting out of my back."

"Well, I think we had better see someone about it, has soon as we are dressed, we will go.

They both go towards Professor Doyle's Office, and they enter, where Professor Doyle was sitting looking at his notes, looks up and spoke.

"Good morning, Janice and John, just the people I would like a word with." John stands there and takes off his shirt and tells the Professor.

"Have you ever seen anything like this." John shrugs his shoulders and these two large wings appear and John spreads them wide, and the Professor sits back in his chair and looking at John who stood there with these two large wings with all the colours of the rainbow, shimmering in the morning light."

Professor Doyle takes off his glasses and tells John.

"This confirms what I thought."

"What are you on about Sir, what you thought.

"I've been looking at you blood tests and reports, and you've just confirmed to me that they are true."

Janice looking at John and seeing for the first time with these wings fully deployed and she turns to Professor Doyle and asking him.

"I`m the same, is it to do with these Aliens that are causing us to change."

"Yes. Janice you`ve hit the nail on the head, for you see, your test yesterday shows that your D.N.A, is changing, it must be with the device in your head."

"That cannot be true, for they told us that they had turned the thing off in our heads." Janice suddenly screams out and she too squeezes her shoulders together, and she no more takes of her top and the same, these two wings pop out and start to spread open, with Janice looking at John and telling him.

"This cannot be happening; I mean unlike yourself John I've had no pain."

"It could be that with you being a female, your hormones must be slightly different from males.

"What are we going to do, I mean we cannot live the rest of our lives like this, they will put us into a freak show, and people will come from around the world to ogle over us, no I don't want to live like that." Janice standing there and starting to sob. John goes over to her and tells her.

"Come on Babe we still have the two of us, we will find a way to overcome this."

"That's the way John, think positive thoughts, you still have us to fall back on."

CHAPTER 18

Janice tells John that she would like to get some fresh air, John looks at the Professor who just nods his head and tells John.

"Please go and take Janice outside, she may settle down with a little Sunshine on her back, sorry about the pun." John does go and Janice and John go and sit next to a lake that was in the Uni grounds. Just before they went outside Janice back in her room cuts a slit in one of her tops, so the wings could protrude when she wanted to spread them and John too, had a T-shirt with a slit in the back. They sit talking for a while and you can imagine what it was about, yes, the predicament that they were in, when along the lakes path come about six students on their way to class, when one of the boys sees the slit in Janice's top, and Johns too, and he comments.

"What have we here two students making a new fashion design." Well, this made then all start to laugh aloud, this infuriated Janice, who just stood and said to them.

"NO. not a modern design, but for these." Janice shrugs her shoulders, and these two large wings open, and this made one or two of them scream, with one saying as they ran away.

"she's an angel, look at those wings, she looks like a butterfly."

"Janice put them away, you will have all of the Uni`s security staff after us."

"Sorry John it was the way they laughed at us, come let's get out of here and go and have a coffee in our room."

They are having their coffee when there is a knock at the door and John goes and answers the door and it was one of Professors Assistants, he asks John.

"The Professor would like you to come to his office."

"Thanks, we will be there in a moment, just finishing our drink and we will be there." They do finish their drink and go to the Professors office, and they go in and sit down and the Professor tells them.

"I must say that you have certainly stirred up a can of worms, for all-around the Uni, is that six students have seen an angel down by the lake."

"That be Janice, for they walked by us and one of them was mocking us, and this infuriated Janice, and I don't have to tell you what happened next."

We will try and calm it down, but in the meantime, we would like to full fill a few more tests on you, then we should have our results, and what to do next. Janice and John sit there just nodding their heads at what Professor had told them, over the next few hours they are subjected to more X-rays and scans, till at lunch time they are told that they could get something to eat. Janice and John go walking off towards the Uni canteen, they get their meal and go and sit at a window overlooking the large lawn of the University complex. Janice asks John.

"What are they going to achieve by all of these tests, I mean it is the Aliens that have caused this, and they will be the only ones who can reverse this."

"We must give them a chance, maybe they will come up with an answer."

"All well, but what if they don't, will we turn completely into those Aliens, I`m frightened John, of what might be, and what the future holds for us." John reaching out for Janice's hand and reassures her.

"Don't give up yet sweetheart, let's just wait and see what they're finding are."

After lunch Janice and John are back in the Professor office and he starts by telling them.

"We have now finished all of our tests, and here are the answers to your tests." Professor Doyle picking up the paperwork off his desk and starts reading the results.

"First off, your blood samples show no sign of admiralties within the cells of your blood, secondly the x-ray on your bone structure specially in the back and spinal cord show a natural growth, and rapid growth of muscle tissue around the wings, which have formed onto the shoulder blades."

"But what about the rest of us, those Aliens had four legs, we are not going to develop legs two are we." Janice looking at the Professor with concern.

"No, my child there is no sign of this happening, and if you are worried, you will not change any other part of your anatomy, it seems it his concentrated around your back." John holding Janice's hand asked the Professor.

"What about operating on us to remove these from our backs, is that possible to do."

"I`m afraid not, already the development and the muscle growth, would make it highly dangerous, with nerves and other issues within the structure of the wings, it's not the sort of thing that had been attempted before." John finally asked the Professor.

"You are telling us that we have to live the rest of our lives with these things on our back."

"I`m afraid so, you must keep them under control and not to expose them in public, for you have already witnessed what they can cause."

Chapter 19

Janice and John spend two more nights at the special unit within the Uni and they are told they can leave. Janice and John are sitting in the carpark and Janice asks John.

"What are we going to do John, I don't feel like going home like this, my Mum, it will kill her if she found out we had been abducted by Aliens." starts to sob, with John telling her.

"Come on now, you are supposed to be my rock, if you are down what Am I supposed to do."

I`m sorry John but it is just all that we have gone through, you know Aliens then these so-called wings, it is getting to much."

"Well, we came here to look at the lakes, so we will jolly well Finnish what we started out to do, so chin up and let's hit the road to the highlands of Scotland, Hawkeye the knew."

Janice laughs at what John had said, and she tells him.

"Your right Babe, so foot down and let's give Scotland what us Midlander's can do, drive on my hero." John blowing Janice a kiss as he pulls out onto the road and starts to head for the highlands of Scotland. They had been driving for about two hours and come to a spot secluded from the road in a valley by a lock that had blue waters and large mountain range and John pulls up and tells Janice.

"This looks fine, no one around just us and the wildlife of Scotland." The Sun high in the sky and the sound of the birds singing their daily chorus made them forget about what had happened, and John setting out the table and chairs gets two drinks out of the fridge plonks them down on the table and tells Janice.

"Here Babe a toast, to us, may the sun never stop shining." They both pick up their glasses with Janice leaning back in her chair and telling John.

"We will be OK wont we John."

"Get that drink down you and fetch the bottle out of the fridge, it's a good drink we want, not negative thoughts." Janice smiles at John and goes and does fetch the bottle of white wine, after they had had a few drinks and Janice with all the prodding and test she did back at the Uni labs, tells John with having a few drinks that she was going to have a nap, to sober up a little, she goes and goes into the bedroom in the motorhome, and she was soon off fast asleep.

She had been asleep for about an hour and a half, when she opens her eyes and all that she sees is the top of the trees, for she had come out of the motorhome and only spread her wings and that is why she was high in the sky, she suddenly screams out loud at being so high, and panics and starts to fall with her wings folding upwards as she fell, then suddenly she is in the arms of John who had flown up and caught her, she is clinging on to John like grim death, and she asks John.

How did I get up here?"

"You must have been sleep walking, but in your case sleep flying. Janice looking at Johns wings that were going ten to the dozen, making the noise just like the Aliens did when flying. They both come back down to the ground and John tells her to open her wings fully, which she does and now he tells her.

"Right start to flap them and build up speed." Janice does this and John holding her hand just said.

"Now lift off the ground," and she does this and with the two of them flying, now they do sound just like the Aliens sounded like when they first visited them in their motorhome. Now Janice is starting to enjoy the experience of flying so much that she swoops down skimming the water's edge, and she is whooping it up, when John to the water's edge and in a clearing sees this man taking photos of Janice frolicking about, John shouts to her saying.

"Janice come down now you are being watched, please babe come now." Janice does what John had said, and she asks him.

"Do you think he will report us."

"Well, you know what people are like today, they will do anything for a quick buck, but do not you worry sweetheart, it is his problem not ours, come lets us pack up and go somewhere else. They start to pack their things away into the garage and secure things inside for the off and taking their seats Janice asks John.

"We are not going to be like this for the rest of our life's are we, you know running away every time we are spotted."

"I suppose it will take a while for people to get use to us, but they will soon get use to us, and things should get back to normal, but we must be weary of people for now, for you never know if we are caught in the wrong place at the wrong time."

"What do you mean caught in the wrong time." John driving off and lifting his hand in the shape of a gun and going BANG. Looking at Janice who looks back at John and just said.

"They would not do a thing like that, would they. All that John did was nod his head up and down.

They had been on the road for about an hour and are by now well into the wilderness and John pulls up at the bottom of this mountain with a small stream running through the valley, he pulls up and tells Janice.

"This looks like a quiet spot; off the beaten track we will camp here."

CHAPTER 20

They set up Camp and settle down around the stream and Janice brings out a coffee for John and sits down looking at the stream trickling by, and the sound of it makes the whole place tranquil. John with a big intake of breath and telling Janice.

"Peace at last, not a sole, but the sheep on the mountain side, and I do not have to tell you that they will not bother us. He had just said this when from the back of the motorhome comes a sheep with her young Lamb, bleeping. Well, if you could have seen Johns face it was a picture with Janice bursting out laughing.

 Later that day Janice making a salad for their dinner and John adjusting the dish on the top of the motorhome from a swich inside of the van, finds the perfect angle and football is on, and he tells Janice.

"Were in luck we have a perfect picture for the main match tonight." Janice tossing the salad looks at John and spoke.

"Woopy can't wait, who be playing then tonight."

"Man, united v Liverpool 7.30 pm kick off."

"Great I'll try and find a delightful book to read." They are sitting down watching the match and enjoying the salad that Janice had prepared with new potatoes. John with a bottle of beer and Janice with her white wine, and after they both sit back and put their feet up and one of them at least enjoys the match, and you can guess who that might be. They both retire and getting undressed suddenly the whole van lights up, and suddenly the van tilts to one side with John holding onto the toilet side door is saying.

" What is going on." Then the van comes to a rest and John lifts the bedroom curtain blind, and he looks at Janice and tells her.

"We are not in the wild anymore but on the Alien craft."

"What do you mean, not camping." Janice coming round to Johns side of the bed, booking out of the window, and seeing all these little ones flying around outside.

"How is it possible to lift a great massive thing like our motorhome up into the air."

"Well, they have, maybe now we will get some answers." John goes to the door and opens it, and steps out onto the alien craft, and the first thing he does is open his wings, so they are on display, with little ones again coming up to him and caressing him. Next it was Janice who steps down onto the Alien craft and opens her wings and the same as John, Janice had little ones caressing her, and touching her bright coloured wings.

Then the leader of the Aliens comes and approaches Janice and John, and he is taken back at what beholds him and again he first passes one of the white balls to John and one for Janice.

"My you have changed, since we last met, the device should not have given you wings, there must be a malfunction, I will investigate this with my colleagues, but first I must welcome you aboard my craft Puritan and forgive me for the welcome our little ones give you, for they are curious of your looks." John folding down his wings asks Regan.

"What are your intensions on bringing also my motorhome up into your craft."

"No real reason just curiosity into human ways, which is why we are here to study humans from a far." John gives off a chuckle and telling him.

"Our far means what it means far, not on your doorstep."

"Humans have funny ways and words, but forgive me my colleagues are calling me, I'll be right back." Regan leaving John and Janice with the little ones, with Janice telling John.

"These little ones are so cute, just look at the colour of their wings, they are so bright and look just like our butterflies back home."

"They are fine, but we've more important things to deal with right now, what do you think is other members of his crew require him for."

"I DONT KNOW John, but I can tell you, that these little ones are adorable." John looking at Janice and thinking, she will be all over me if he comes back and wants to do more tests on us. Just as John had said this, he does come back with three others, and he comes up to John and through the ball in his hand tells him.

"We have been discussing your welfare and come to the conclusion that if you require the help of us, to remove these wings that have developed on yourself and the female of your species, the only way we could proceed is to go back to our World and preform an operation to safely remove them. So, it is your choice to come or not, Please go with your female partner discuss the matter, and in one Earth hour time, come and give us your answer."

Regan lowers his head towards John turns and all four of them leave John, Who stood there looking at Janice smiling and playing with the little Aliens. John and Janice go back into their motorhome and Janice laughing at being pulled back as she tries to enter the Motorhome.

They finally close the door to their motorhome.

CHAPTER 21

Inside Janice panting with dealing with the little Aliens looks at John and asked him.

"Why have we come into the motorhome, what is the matter."

"It`s their leader Regan, he had put an ultimatum to us."

"And what might that be then." Janice looking at John and waiting for an answer.

"He told me that the only way to remove these wings is, if we go with them to their World and have them preform another operation to remove them, I`ve got to give him an answer in an hour's time. So, what are your thoughts of going to their planet and going ahead with the procedure that they want to perform on us."

"Well, I`m not sure right now, in a way I`m glad I have them when around the Aliens, but not comfortable around my friends and other humans, what about yourself John, what are your feelings on going and having them removed."

I`m the same as you Janice, I to do like them, and especially when flying around, just like a bird, free and up in the air, seeing the World at a different angle."

"That would be fine, but on the other hand people would look at us in an unusual way, freaks of nature, I mean humans are not to be up in the air, like birds." John holding Janice's hand and telling her.

"We cannot live in two Worlds, so let's get our life's back on track and go and have then removed." John just when the hour is up, calls for Regan to see them, and he does come to Johns motorhome and John comes out and he tells Regan their decision."

"Janice and I have decided to go with you to your planet and have them removed, but if I may You say that you live many light years away, how long the flight to your Planet will be.

Regan tells John.

In your Earth days it will be only fourteen, when we arrive at our home Planet Archon, Our Craft Puritan will safely take us there at our speed."

"What is that speed then."

"We can fly well over the speed of light, in the vacuum of space, I think your Earth scientists call light speed that cannot be surpassed, but your theory of reality is wrong, for we can bend and warp space to reach our goals, much more easily, pleas both come, and I will show you what our spacecraft can do."

Janice and John do go with Regan to a what we would call the control room, where there are Aliens at their posts with what looks like a large window, and Regan is giving out orders to his crew, but Janice and John cannot hear him for he is talking telepathically to them, and not using the ball from around his neck to communicate with Janice and John. He turns to Janice and John and tells them.

"We are ready to jump into a wormhole, you may feel a little jerk and a little nauseous don't worry it will not last long, Regan drops his arm and suddenly there is a jerk and Janice and John looking out of the front window see all these streaks of colour flashing by, and they do feel the effects of it, but just like Regan told them it soon passes.

Over the next fortnight Janice seemed to get on well with the little ones, even to the point where she used her communicator to teach the ways of Earthing's and the games children played in parks and fields upon the Earth. They do spend time around the craft, but still used their Motorhome for when they needed the time for themselves to be alone. One or two nights they dine with Regan, and he shows them the Planet Archon, and clips what we call films of the ways of the Archons.

It's the day they are about to come out of the wormhole and Land on Archon, Janice and John are up in the control room, and once again Regan had taken over the leadership while he directed is crew into home approach, John looking out of the window when Archon comes into view, and he gasps at the size of it, for it must have been three times the size of the Earth, and the colours of the blue and lush green of the land mass, was a site to behold. John terns to Regan and tells him.

"You have certainly had a beautiful Planet."

"Thank you, John, and you will be surprised even more when we land." It`s not long it lands, and John is surprised for it had not landed on the ground but on the top of a skyscraper. Regan tells Janice and John to follow him. They go to an opening in the craft and go walking down this ramp and onto a platform Regan tells Janice and John, look down on your left see the arch halfway down the building that is where we will be going." Janice looks and asks Regan.

"How do we get down there, have you transport.

Regan chuckled at what Janice had said, he opens his wings and starts to flap them at an all-mighty rate and goes up into the air with the rest of his crew and he tells Janice and John, please follow, this may be the last time you will be able to use your wings."

John and Janice do spread their wings and follow Ragan down the skyscraper, with Janice saying to John.

"Listen to the buzzing, it is just like the noise we first heard them coming to our motorhome.

CHAPTER 22

Janice and John landed on the archway, halfway down the skyscraper and looking all round and are just like to explorers who had just discovered a new land, John Holding Janice's hand tells her as they went into the building.

"This is it babe, the next time we come out here we will need transport." Janice just grimmest at John at the thought of not being able to fly again. They are escorted into a room where there are Aliens all in white and one beckons them towards this arm that they had seen before when they first meet the Aliens, back up on their space craft when they first saw the device.

John is the first and this Alien just points this device at them and they both go horizontally up and are lying there next to this arm, and before knew it they were both unconscious, and this arm comes down and starts the operation to remove the wings, they are under for well over 6 hours and they wake up after in this room and this time they were on a bed John looks and Janice whom be next to him, and he smiles at her, and gradually both come round and sit up in bed, and the first thing John said was.

"My back it does not feel any different, John getting out of the bed, and spreading his wings, and Janice the same she too gets out of bed, and does the same, and they both stand there with their colourful wings on full display, when into the room comes Regan with two other Aliens and they approach Janice and John, and the first thing they do is clasp their hands and give their greeting and Regan spoke.

"We and these Physicians who performed the operation, failed on all accounts to remove the wings, but fount the resistance of the human DNA, was overpowering strong, resisting all attempts to rectify the situation. They tried, the bone structure and the main blood vessels just keep reproducing, our nano technology had changed in the human body, which is why we cannot reverse the procedure or remove the wings, one other thing, your strength had increased tenfold. We first notice this when you lifted that motorhome off one of your fellow Earthlings." John just looked at Janice and then back to Regan and spoke.

"You're telling us we have become superheroes, like what we see on movies and TV shows."

"I do not know of these superheroes you mention, but yes you are now different from the rest of your species." Then Janice goes over and holds John and tells him.

"Well at least we now know our future and it will be up to us to make the best of it, I John and will always will, whatever the future holds for us."

"I too Babe love you and will always be here for you." John looking back at Regan and telling him.

"We woke to go home now."

"We will ready our craft for the return to Planet Earth, and once again, we are sorry for the stress and damage we have caused too your body, for this we will forever be by your side in case of any help you may need."

"Thank you. "for your concern."

Over the next few days, they do ready their craft ready for the journey back to the Earth, and Janice and John have been doing a little exploring around the City of Regan's home. They are walking through this large intercity park, with lush trees and plants, not like the ones on Earth but large trees and colours of blue yellow and of course green. John holding Janice's hand, suddenly get this high pitch sound and they both hold their heads, with Janice looking to where the sound is coming from and see`s these little ones that had been playing on this ride that looked like the monkey climber back on Earth, and these little ones trapped underneath the thing that had collapsed, with little ones trapped underneath.

"My God John look." John looks and just tells Janice.

"Come on babe quickly, lets help them." They both go running over to the ride and John on one side and Janice on the other they lift the heavy construction, and these little ones all flutter out of the Monkey climber, Janice and John lower the construction back down and before you know it they both had these little ones coming to them and are being caressed and they were being cling to for comfort, luckily none of the young ones was seriously injured ,thanks to the quick thinking of Janice and John. Within minutes parents of the little ones are flocking to the park with the news of what had happened, and Janice and John are the centre of attention, on what they did.

They arrive back at the tower skyscraper and are approached by this adult Alien who with the white ball communicates with them, and he tells them

"You are needed up on the roof for departure for the return journey back to Earth. Commander Regan is awaiting you." They thank him and make their way to the roof, where the craft is waiting, and might I say this humming sound coming from the craft.

They are welcomed aboard and shown to where Commander Regan be. Commander Regan sitting in his highchair welcomes both and he had been told what had happened on the park early on that day.

"Today you saved the lives of a lot of our young ones, and we are forever grateful on your quick actions

CHAPTER 23

It is another fortnight journey back to Earth and it was on the thirteenth day when they are in the main control room when Commander Regan approaches them and asked.

"Can I have a quick word with you."

"sure, we are all yours." Janice and John approaching Regan, and he tells them.

"There is one thing we forgot to tell you; about the journey you have just undertaken."

"And what might that be." John looking at Regan.

"Have you heard about the reality of evolution, from that well know, and probably the best-known Scientist to man had ever known, Dr Albert Einstein."

"Of course, we have, he talked a lot about speed, and light speed travel, and what would happen if you surpassed the speed of light, one of his best and well known theory of speed and light travel, and what can happen when you travel at the speed of light and time laps, and Oh my God you are not going to tell me that with driving at twice the speed of light when we arrive back on Earth over 500 years will have elapse."

"Sorry yes that is true, for you see it`s the same for us, we chose to travel looking for new life, but we too suffer the same consequences, when we travel back home, the only thing our people know is what is told in our history books, and the signals we transmit on traveling back to our World." Janice asks Regan.

"My Mum you are telling t we have only been away for 4 weeks, and my Mum is now dead, no you are not right, tell him John he`s got all of his facts wrong, hasn't he, please John tell him." John did not know what to say for he knew with studying Einstein at Uni, that Regan was right.

"Sorry Janice, it's true." Janice breaks down and starts to cry, just shouting her Mums name out and saying to herself.

"It`s a dream I'll wake up in a minute." John trying to comfort her, and they both stand looking at the screen showing just these white lines, and one of the crew tells Regan and through one of the white balls so Janice and John could hear.

"Sir dropping out of supersonic speed approaching orbit of the planet Earth."

"Good raise clowning shield and maintained orbit." Regan tells Janice and John that it is time to say goodbye, and sincerely I do regret that you will have to start a new life here on Earth, I wish you both good fortune in the future, from myself and my crew I wish you goodbye."

"Regan standing and lowering his head to Janice and John who make their way to where their motorhome be, and of course they are escorted to their motorhome by the ones who be caressing them, yes the little ones, and John enters first with once again Janice stroking their little heads and stepping onto the step of the motorhome and turning, and closes the door and the first thing she does his put her arms around John, and John the same and he gives her one big hug and kiss and telling her.

"We will be fine Janice, at least we have each other. They are sitting at the front of the van with John in the driving seat and Janice sitting next to him, and then suddenly the whole of the windscreen goes bright white, and they feel a little sway and then the white from the windscreen clears and they see one of the locks water flickering in the sunlight. John looks at Janice and tells her.

"We are home Babe are you ready to go." All that Janice said was.

"Home, don't you mean 2522, 500 years what hell are we going to find."

"Well should we head for home and see what we find first, then we will decide what to do."

"Whatever, but" Janice is about to continue but stops dead at seeing this craft on the water, but not on the water but above it about four feet and going extremely fast.

"Look John that boat, it's in the air."

"Wow if this is what we are going to find, then we are going to look out of place traveling in this thing." John pulling onto the road, he had been going for about ten minutes when this sports car goes by him and John comments to Janice.

"Did you see that, Babe; they must be the all-electric cars." John had noticed that when people were walking by, they were getting some strange looks. He had been on a motorway for about two hours, and he tells Janice that they will pull into a service station, He pulls in and the first thing that he noticed was instead of pumps for petrol or diesel, there were electrical points where you see cars pulling into them, plugging in and about ten minutes unplugging fully charged, John turns to Janice and tells her.

"Look Janice they charge up within ten minutes sure is an improvement from our days." John had not seen this guy coming over to him and he asks John.

"Excuse me for asking, where did you get the campervan from, it must be well over five hundred years old, and it looks brand new. "

John looking at him and he tells him."

"Why thanks, and yes, it is brand new, I've only had it for just over two months, by the way it's not a campervan, but a motorhome." John smiling at him.

"Can you answer me a question." John asking the man.

"Sure, what might it be."

"Do they still serve diesel."

"only at special stations, and you're in luck, for if you go round to the side, you will see one of the old type pumps, but it`s quite expensive."

"Thanks for that." Then John realised that he did not have any money on him, and he knew that his cards would not work, and he is glad that he filled up before the Aliens abducted them. John looks at Janice and tells her.

"Come on Babe we had better go back to our van and put the kettle on, for we cannot use the services."

"Why not, we are as good as anyone else."

"We might be, but for one thing."

"And what might that be." Janice giving John that look that seemed to say what are you on about.

"We`ve not got any money to pay for it."

"Oh yes I see."

"Come on then let's go, and then we will continue our journey."

They go walking back and do have coffee, and a few biscuits, with people walking bye to the services and giving them a look at their motorhome, and Janice and John at the table drinking coffee.

CHAPTER 24

They travel for well over 7 hours and do pull up outside Janice's house, but to their surprise, it no longer existed, instead there was a block of skyscrapers, and Janice looking up to them and saying.

"Oh, Mum I`m so sorry. What are we going to do John, we've no money, and nowhere to live"?

"We will soon have money mark my word, and for somewhere to live, Dah-dar." John pointing to the bedroom then back to Janice."

"Point taken, come on then let's turn in, for its been a long day today with all the driving that you have done." John pulls up in the skyscrapers carpark and parks at the edge out of the way, and he pulls down all the blinds to make it more secure, and so not one can investigate the inside of the motorhome, they took in and are soon off into the land of the nod. The next mornig it was up wash shower and shave, and while they were eating Breakfast Janice asked John.

"Well, what's this money-making scheme you were on about last night."

"Firstly, we will go to the local paper with our story of being abducted by Aliens, and it will soon get round, and before you know it, they will be throwing money at us."

"Don`t be so silly, who would buy our story."

"Trust me Babe, just wait and see, drink up and let's get down there." Janice shaking her head at Johns foolish idea, does drink up and before you know it John is driving off for the City centre, and the looks he gets as he drives into the City centre; he finds the local paper and pulls up in the carpark, and stepping down from the motorhome is confronted by the papers security guard.

"What have we here, Doctor Who and his side kick, you cannot park there my friend, this is a private carpark."

"John looking at him and telling him.

"You're good, I mean in a way we are Doctor Who and his side kick, for we are over 500 years of age, and this is our home the motorhome, we had been abducted by Aliens and want to share it with the World, and I think one of your editors might be interested." Janice looking at John realised now what

Johns scheme was, to sell their story, to the press, she is about to tell John when this man in a suit comes over and spoke.

"What have you here Bill." (Bill is the security guard.)

"Good morning, Sir, apparently these two strangers say they were abducted by Aliens and would like to know if we would be interested."

"Not more of these freaks, sorry but we are up to our ears in tails of Aliens and flying saucers."

"Freaks how dear you, we are not kidding you, we were abducted and did the rest of these freaks do this." John turning to Janice as his wings start to come out and all he tells her is.

"Do what I do sweetheart." John fully brings out his wings and stands there gently flapping them, and Janice the same, with both the security guard and the man in a suit step back at seeing this display by John and Janice.

"My God, you are truly telling me the truth, please be putting those things away and follow me, Bill watch over their thing, whatever it be.

"It's our home a 2022 model Motorhome, it's over 500 years old."

They are taken to this Office and after a few minutes the Editor of the newspaper comes in and he address Janice and John.

"Good morning, one of my associates told me that you have a story to tell about being abducted by Aliens and want to sell your story, well we are not in the position to buy such an important thing like this, but before you say anything, I`ve already spoken to one of my associates at a big London consortium, and what I`ve told them, and what has happened to you they are willing to offer you a six figure sum for the whole story. That is if this figure is to your approval." John looking at Janice and asking her.

"What do you think Babe, should we take the offer."

"Yes, I think so." Janice hardly containing herself, for inside of her head she was jumping up and down and saying YES."

"OK you're on, what do we have to do."

"Well, you can start by telling me the whole story, and from the beginning, my secretary who will be here shortly, and then we can begin." While we wait, what is it about these wings that you have, could you show me them. John standing and looking up to the ceiling and the walls, tells the Editor.

"I'll try but it might be to small Mr, I don`t think we've been introduced yet."

"So sorry forgive me, I`m the editor of the morning news Mr Richard Richmond, and you may be."

"John Blackmore, and this is my partner, Janice." Introductions over and John does partly open his wings and the Editor inspects them and saying.

"My they are so beautiful, and the muscle around the wings looks mighty strong."

CHAPTER 25

"You will get to know more about them as the story unfolds." Just then with Johns wings taking much of the room, into the room comes the editors secretary and she gives of one big scream at seeing a man with wings.

"Mrs Brooks there is no need to worry, he will not hurt you." John folding down is wings and starting to look like a normal man, with Mrs Brooks going and sitting next to The Editor, taking out her shorthand machine and telling Mr Richmond that she was ready.

"Right first off, I must first tell you that everything you tell me will be published by my own paper and transferred to my associate who will be the main buyer of the exclusive story of the obduction, of two humans and the effects that have happened, and of course the fascinating story of time travel that had occurred." John butts in asking him.

"You say you will print the story, but how can it be exclusive if you are selling it on to a third party, surely, he would not be happy knowing that you have printed said story.

"Oh I`m sorry when I told you my associate, he be a partner of the same company as mine, so in layman's terms whatever my paper make out of the story, we both will benefit with being partners, so do not worry we will arrange payment as soon as you have fulfilled your story to us. Hopes this clears up the matter about third party involvement." John just shrugging his shoulders.

"Right from the beginning start your story.

John begins from the beginning when he first brought the motorhome. They both had been telling the story for well over four hours and Mr Richmond puts up his hand and tells them.

"It`s 1pm, I think we will knock off for lunch, for I bet Mrs Brooks fingers are sore. Mr Richmond looking at Mrs Brooks who just lifts her eyebrows at his comment. They do break up and Janice and John are shown to the newspapers restaurant, where they are served at table service with waitresses dressed in black skirts with a white apron, it is the first time Janice and John had seen such service that seemed to go back to their own time only seen in posh establishments. They are given menus and Johns eyes light up when he looks at the menu, for what he was looking at is rump steak, only £52.00, he shows Janice who just tells him.

"Don`t forget John, you won't get one for £6.80, for that was 500 years ago."

"Bloody inflation, don't think I want to know our much chips cost."

"Just get what you want, we are not paying for it." Janice smiling at the waitress and telling her.

"I'm sorry about that, Mr Richmond told us to order what we like and to put it on his account. Well, what a difference what Janice had said, and John sitting upright and telling the waitress.

"In that case I had better have ribeye steak chips and plenty of bread and butter if you please."

They enjoy their posh meal and after resume in Mr Richmond office and continue to tell him about the rest of the abductions and the journey to the Planet Archon, for the failure of their operation to remove their wings. Then Mr Richmond asks John.

"How come it took you 500 years to return, why aren't you dead, I mean 500 years, and you said you were only away for 14 days." Mr Richmond sitting there looking puzzled at Johns answer.

"The only thing I can ask you is look it up on the internet."

"What the hell are you on about, the internet went out over 400 years ago." Janice and John looking at each other than Janice asks him.

"What do you use for communicate with others on the planet, if you don`t have internet."

"Just one of these," Mr Richmond pulling out what looks like a mobile, then clipping it back onto his belt.

"How does it word, I mean if someone sends you an e-mail how do you see what they have put."

My you`ve a lot to learn about modern day technology."

"If someone leaves you a message just say message." Then Mr Richmond hears someone

say, "good morning, Richard." Quickly he just
said. "end call."

"You`ll soon pick it up, "Right now we will get
down to payment, we have come to a figure of
£102100, if you agree to this sum, just sign
here." Janice and John do sign the contract,
and Mr Richmond passes John a card and
telling him.

"If you take this next door to international
banking company, they will transfer it into an
account for you. We have your details and will
be in touch with you, here is two new
telecoms, set up and ready to use, if any
difficulties just pop into reception and they will
be clad to help you with any enquiries, till later
Janice and John, I thank you for using us for
your story.

They go and straight to next door and deposit
their card that Mr Richmond gave them.

CHAPTER 26

They are back at their motorhome and Janice aske John.

"Well, what now, did you notice on the way home everyone was looking at us."

"I think with us travelling in a 500-year-old vehicle, no wonder where getting looks, we will have to change it, if we want to stay anonymous." Janice goes outside and she unfolds her wings and flutters them, when John comes out and sees her standing there, and straight away tells her.

"Janice what do you think you are doing, if anyone see`s you" But he was to later for there was about six youths walking along a towpath beside the canal that ran along the side of the skyscrapers, and they all start to wolf whistle and one or two shouting.

"Look over their an angel or is she an overgrown pigeon. They start to come over to where they were, and one lad picks up a brick and throws it towards Janice, who manages to catch it with her hand. John is shouting to them.

"Back off lads we don`t want any trouble." He starts to unfold his wings and he too now stands with them spread open, and the Lads still advanced towards them chanting their war song. John looks at Janice and just said.

"Now look what you`ve done, whatever they do don`t hurt them." One of the Lads heard what John had said and he tells his mates."

"Let's show these pair of birds what we do to people like them come on let's get them. "They start to charge Janice and John, John picks two of them up by the scruff of their necks and fly's up into the air and dumps them into the canal, with Janice following up and the same dumping them into the canal. Janice and John watch them swimming to the edge of the canal and trying to pull themselves out, through the thick mud. The smell is horrendous with the water being stagnant, John and Janice come flying down and land not to close and asks them.

"Do you need more or are you now satisfied that we do not intend you any arm."

"Please Mr we don't want any more trouble honest." The Lad standing and trying to wipe the stinking mud of himself, and a couple were shredding one or two tears, off what had happened, John turns to Janice and he tells her.

"Come on Babe let's find somewhere else to camp, for we don`t want to have them coming back in the dead of night and getting up to mischief while we sleep." The four Lads watch them as they pull out of the carpark and they travel just out of town into a lay-by that is set back behind some large bushes and out of sight of the road, they settle down for the night and Janice laying in bed asks John.

"What's going to happen to us John, I mean we have no friends for they are all gone, no future." John stops her and tells her.

"Come on now babe we have each other that is the main thing, and as for the future, it`s how we make it, not the way it bestowed upon us, so come on think of wonderful things in your dreams and let them happen." This seemed to calm Janice and she was soon off into sweet dreams and before you know it it's the next morning and Janice wakes up to the smell of breakfast cooking. She sits up stretches and looks at John standing over the stove and tells John.

"You're up early, and that smells nice."

"Well get yourself up and I will start to plate up this gorgeous breakfast."

All done and they both enjoy their breakfast with John telling her.

"What we will do is go and get some money out of the ATM, then go and explore this new World that we are starting out in."

They are off and pull up at a supermarket, John draws money out then they go and John pops into a news agency and picks up the Morning newspaper. He looks at it and his face lights up where on the front page, he see`s himself and Janice standing there with their wings outstretched, and the headlines are.

Couple abducted by Aliens and now have wings and have been transported 500 years into the future. John showing Janice the paper, she`s about to say something to John when from behind a gentleman with a paper shout out.

"It's that couple that are in the paper, where are your wings."

"John grabs Janice's hand and tells her.

"Come on babe before we have a crowd, surrounding us. They go hurriedly to their motorhome and pulling out of the carpark there are one or two people pointing to their motorhome and John saying to Janice.

"God did they have to tell people in the paper that we had this 500-year-old motorhome, now we will be recognised by everyone."

"We`ll head for the coast and hide, for a while."

"Oh, John its turning into a nightmare from hell."

CHAPTER 27

John pulls into a small off-road disused site that once had a house on it that had been pulled down and the area flattened. John looking round tells Janice.

"We will stop here for a while, till the news story dies down or we get kicked off. That evening, they are watching a little tv and have a drink, when from outside the area is lit up with this bright light, John lifting the blind that was next to the window where they were sitting and all that he could see was this white light, and Janice asking John.

"They are back John, it's the Aliens." John looking at Janice and had nothing to say for he knew she was right, and the next thing they know there is a knock at the door, and John goes and opening the door and standing there bowing his head is Regan holding out this white ball, with John taking it and Regan tells John.

"We have been monitoring you and we think it is our fault that you are getting all the wrong publicity with being outsiders, and my fellow top scientises have come up with a theory, that with traveling at the speed of light, you are repelled into the future, but we have found a way to reverse time and travel in a reverse speed to travel back in time. So, in theory we could take you back to your time, but there is a problem, for we are too large that is our craft, so therefore, we have a smaller craft that will only be large enough for yourself and you so-called Motorhome, if you would like to undertake the journey."

"Oh, John let's do it, for I would be able to see my Mum and our friends again, Home, please John."

"What are the risks that we face." Regan looks at them both and just said.

"There are risks at everything one undertakes, even us when we first set out in search of other life forms have to undertake risks, like our own home times, until now we cannot travel back to our own times, for we have been on a long mission, and our time back home had moved on, but if this works then even, we might be able to go home to the times we know and not the future." Janice and John agree to take the risk, and Regan steps back and this sound and suddenly they are in a room and all that they hear is this automated voice telling them.

"Strap into your seat and hold tight, journey begins in in thirty seconds earth time." Janice and John hurriedly fasten themselves into the motorhome seats and Janice reaches out her hand for John to hold." Then this voice tells them.

"10-9- 8-7-64-3-2-1-0 jump into hyper drive started, John sits there and it was if his head was going to explode with Janice squeezing Johns hand, and the same she is trying to look at John, all that she sees is John, who looks like he was fading in and out, she is trying to say something but nothing is coming out, then in a flash it felt like they were breaking at an almighty pace then there was silence, and Janice asking John.

"What is happening John."

"I don't know sweetheart, what's that noise." Suddenly there is this whirling sound and Janice and John look out of the windscreen window, and it suddenly goes bright, and they were standing on Janice's driveway. Janice looks out of the window and sees her Mum coming towards the van, and screams out just saying Mum-Mum, she's out of her seat and goes running towards the door, she jumps down the steps and grabs hold of her Mum, and telling her she loves her so much, with John coming to the door and she looks at John and spoke.

"What have you done to her, I thought you were going to Scotland today.

"We where Mum but I`ve changed my mind, and we are off to Devon and Cornwall. John touching his back and no wings, for they had come back to the time before they had even met the Aliens.

THE END

OR

IS IT.

Thanks for reading this story of Caressed by a butterfly hopes you enjoyed it, maybe I will do a follow up, so keep your eyes open, this is my 54th book.

by

John Bolstridge.

www.ingramcontent.com/pod-product-compliance
Lightning Source LLC
Chambersburg PA
CBHW061540120726

48001CB00004B/1650